The Waiting Room

The Waiting Room

by Anne Dandurand

Translated by Robert Majzels

THE MERCURY PRESS

The publisher gratefully acknowledges the financial assistance of the Canada Council for the Arts and the Ontario Arts Council. The publisher further acknowledges the financial support of the Government of Canada through the Book Publishing Industry Development Program (BPIDP) for its publishing activities.

Canadä

The author wishes to thank Wolfgang Amadeus Mozart for the unspeakable.

Edited by Beverley Daurio
Composition and page design by TASK
Printed and bound in Canada
1 2 3 4 5   03 02 01 00 99

Canadian Cataloguing in Publication Data
Dandurand, Anne, 1953-
[Salle d'attente. English]   The waiting room
Translation of: La salle d'attente.
ISBN 1-55128-073-6
I. Majzels, Robert, 1950- . II. Title.
PS8557.A52S2413 1999   C843'.54   C99-932062-9
PR3919.2.D247S2513 1999

The Mercury Press 22 Prince Rupert Avenue
Toronto, Ontario CANADA M6P 2A7

The cat is a whirling dervish until the milk arrives.
— Bengali proverb

[...] sexually, that is to say, with my soul [...]
— Boris Vian, The Red Grass

I

ALLEGRO FURIOSO

On the ceiling, fluorescent lights. On the wall, a No Smoking sign. Around the edges of the room, metal chairs covered in a cinereous plastic. Everything here, in this underground clinic next to the subway, is gray, winter gray, wretched gray. Outside, inside, the same melancholy, the same gloom.

A receptionist goes about her business; you can hear the sounds of her fluty voice and paper shuffling behind the counter. On the edge of his seat, a young South American nervously fingers a tattered medical insurance card. A little further down, a bum, stinking of piss and booze, nods in his seat. Over by the shelf cluttered with leaflets, a young woman frets behind lowered eyelids. No fair Hebe this, her bony frame disguised in shapeless sweaters, her drab hair cut in an unruly mop. Her hands would be pretty were they not so disfigured by her nails, arched, carnelian and far too long.

She grits her teeth. A long-time asthma sufferer obliged to renew her prescription at every change of season, she despises the waste of time; she switches clinics from one prescription to the next, in a vain attempt to vary her displeasure. Though she appears relaxed, she remains alert. She knows me, knows I'll take advantage of her boredom to invade her. I've been torturing her for a good twenty of her thirty-five years. No one can see me: just another succubus. A ghoul. A voice only she can hear. I chose her because the flows of her desire never rise to the crater's lips.

I remember the very first night I introduced myself

to her. We were in the depths of one of those vacant Februarys when one prefers to doze on into warming April. She was almost fifteen and had been crying herself to sleep again, weeping over her weedy and stubbornly child-like silhouette. Sorrow at that age always seems so irreparable. I sent her the dream of a bouquet of scarlet anthuriums, each obscene golden pistil pulsating and greedy, as it rose from a single petal. In her dream, the spray had flared between her thighs, thighs as yet unbroached by any man's hand, and the heady scent, a tinge of something fetid, had wrapped round her like the monsoon's damp silk embrace. How I gloried then, in her moaning, and later, in her morning confusion.

Her eyes have settled on the receptionist. My turn to sing.

I need only slip a single phrase into her mind: *What if you wanted her?* and she's done for. She knows I'm about to bewitch her. She stiffens. Fights to resist me. And yet, with me, against me, she has tasted nothing but defeat. Condemned to death, how can she even think to oppose an immortal? I am aroused by the murmurings of her struggle. I nuzzle a cheek, her lashes tremble, I nip at the nape of her neck, I know every secret to enthrall her. Below, already, her nymphs are all aquiver.

— And what if you'd been in love with this woman for a long time? Spellbound by her honeysuckle scent, her damp odour, you long to drown yourself in it, can't bear to be deprived of it. You wait until no one is watching, step behind the counter. Puma of desire, cobra of love, that's what you've become. The secretary says nothing, the gleam in your eye tells her what you want. You kneel between her knees. You slip a hand beneath her lilac skirt, take hold of the crotch of her pink panties and slide them off. She edges forward on her chair to help you. You're in no hurry. You can't resist nozzling her thong. You know she wants you,

too, although she attends to her business as though nothing were happening, as though her nylon stockings could prevent your kisses stirring her fires. Faced with her feigned indifference, you decide to make her cry out, here, in front of all these strangers.

First, with your nails, you sketch nerve-wracking furrows up from her ankles to the soft flesh of her thighs; then, with your thumbs, you spread her labia. Beneath the lilac skirt, they glow crimson, and you exult in this instantaneous response to your touch. The one you want answers the phone and, to break her resistance, you thrust your index roughly into her cleft, marvelling at how quickly she moistens. Slowly you explore, you can feel the one you want resisting, resisting this sensation welling up inside her. On a whim, just to delay her pleasure, you remove your finger as brutally as you inserted it. You cool her off even more with a quick bite, leaving the imprint of your canines on her groin, a tattoo of your love. You tug her pubic hair through your teeth, thrust your tongue into the breach of her sex, you flirt with her clitoris, just lightly enough to exasperate her; she swings her hips forward, offering herself to you and, without stirring, your gums can feel her blood seethe. At last, to quicken the pace, you wrap your mouth around her petioles and you devour her...

Overwrought, my victim leaps from her seat, runs across to the pamphlets, grabs one and sits down again, all this far too quickly to conceal her distress. The pamphlet is about condoms. It contains neither photos nor illustrations. Boring. You're mine, my little doe, all mine. Cruelty is a delicious candy, to be sucked slowly.

— If you truly loved each other, at the end of your lives you would still love each other forever and ever. Today will be the thirtieth anniversary of your relationship. Now you are grown old, but the fervor in

your hearts burns unabated. Springtime, the first afternoon of a precocious spring: the city sheds its old hide, bare necks offer themselves to a warm sun, everything is bathed in the light of deliverance.

Having scrubbed down your apartment in readiness for the return of the buds and crows, you've set out for that country cottage where, together over the years, you've whiled away so many peaceful hours. In the car, she holds your hand while she drives; you are listening to Brahms at full volume, concerto number 2 in B flat, opus 83; the allegro appassionato washes over you both in all its furor, stirring your imaginations: suddenly, you are back in the eighteenth century, two wealthy young ladies of noble birth, each astride her spirited sorrel. Following a wild gallop beside a still unclouded river, you have slowed your charges to a walk and entered the undergrowth of a wood in Sologne where, intoxicated by the lathered necks of your stallions and the sharp aroma of the surrounding tender greenery, you tie your mounts to an oak and rush into each other's arms, into the rustle of your many-coloured satin dresses, while your steeds, standing over your precise caresses, prick up their ears at the sound of sapphic groaning. Imagining all this together in the car on the way to your country house, the shared fantasy, entwined with the concerto, has tousled the white mane of your sixty years.

At the cottage, the tits and woodpeckers are in open-throated song, the lake is cracking free from its winter fetters, even the icicles on the edge of the roof are gleaming their last tears. Inside, a birch fire burns pale beneath the light of triumphant day. Easily, with that perfect harmony of movement which comes only after thirty years of intimacy, you cook your anniversary meal: oysters stuffed with star anise and Pineau des Charentes, cushion of beef Wellington stuffed with foie gras and diced mushrooms, and for dessert, tsarinas, those shortbread pastries sprinkled with raisins *soaked in rum. Sipping your Veuve-Clicquot and savouring your meal by candlelight, you bandy smutty remarks back and forth, giggling like schoolgirls sharing a cigarette on the sly. After your coffee, she comes to you with a strange smile. She says: "I have something for you, do you want it?" and since you do, she adds: "I have to tie you up before I can give it to you. Do you still want it?" She's loved you too long for you to fear anything coming from her, but a kind of exquisite trepidation presses against your chest. Arms entwined about waists, pecking and smooching, you make your way up to your mottled aquamarine attic. She commands you to stop fidgeting as she places five church candles at the head of the bed; she whispers a command to lie down, naked, and to keep your arms and legs spread wide. You blush to see yourself this way, old wrinkled carcass, like flabby meat on display in a butcher shop; you find yourself incapable of interpreting the smile of the one who loves you as she binds your feet and wrists with silk scarves to the posts of your bed. You laugh nervously at the pleasure of this forced powerlessness, already your vulva grows damp, "Too soon, too fast," she who loves you scolds with mock severity. Standing next to you, inscrutable, she looks you over, and the air in the room grows heavy. With a flourish she uncorks a dull blue-green glass bottle you have never seen, tilts the bottle over your sternum, pours a thin line of liquid cream from which you can make out the smell of oranges and Cayenne pepper, spreads the cream down to your belly and, without lingering there, moves on to each of your legs. Now she massages methodically, too methodically, each of your toes, each arch, each ankle, moves up to your calves, your knees, your thighs, you beg her now to seize your bush, to ravish you, but, in an unrecognizable and frightening voice, she debates whether it might not be better to gag you in order to shut you up. You promise silence, and resigning yourself to the inescapable, turn your head to the milky moonlight streaming through the window. Against the glass, the bittersweet nightshade is not yet in bloom, a few tiny crimson clusters cling stubbornly to dry branches. The one you love is working on your hips now, your ribs, your arms, kneading you to the tips of your fingers. She has passed over your breasts, but you have abandoned all protest; instead, you relish your surrender. There is nothing, nothing you can do: more vulnerable than an infant stripped of its swaddling clothes, you feel an entirely new, or perhaps very ancient, joy fill your lungs.*

The one who loves you is leaving, you don't dare ask why. You wait. You languish. Almost dozing. Outside, a capricious gust of wind whips through the trees, an army of nimbus clouds assaults the sky. Suddenly, a burning sensation, from your shoulders to your toes: the Cayenne pepper in the cream, the cream applied with such minute attention! Your breasts, by contrast, and your pubes are rimed stone, shards of marble...

Can the one who loves you have forgotten you? Rejected you? She may have fled under cover of the wind. If she has truly left you here for good, no one will come to your rescue, you'll not be able to untie yourself, you'll die in unbearable agony. Your skin is in flames. The gift of cruel death, by thirst and fire. Despair shatters you.

Suddenly a cascade of water hammers the windowpanes, lightning slashes the night, a storm breaks, batters the house, raging. A shutter in the living room begins to flap, beating stubbornly against your anxious heart. A heavy step, too heavy to belong to the one who loves you, advances toward the garret. A giant crosses the threshold. His head concealed beneath a terrifying beaked mask of leather, he raises his arms toward you, his immense cloak of tufted feathers unfurls, you can't believe your eyes, he approaches the

bed, steps across you, lowers himself between your
knees, his buskin boots scraping against your shins,
you can't quite make out his body beneath the mass
of his robe, but, between the folds, a monstrous ebony
phallus juts forward at you. The colossus bears down,
hesitating for an instant on the lip of your crevice, and
you shiver at the shaft's first graze, the cold touch of
oiled wood. The fragrance of honeysuckle suddenly fills
your nostrils. Behind the mask, you discover the pure,
so pure, almost transparent azure of the eyes of the
one you love, you can't quite believe this gift she is
offering you, she plunges into you, impales you, your
mind reels, Zeus blazes in your womb, you are Leda
heaving in orgasms, and the one who loves you is in
you, and I too am in you, libidinal trinity, triangle of
fire spinning in a storm-torn sky, until finally you
surrender, nothing, nothing, you are absolutely nothing, perhaps the one who loves you has tunneled an
escape through your womb into infinity, perhaps at

last you have freed me, your chimera, perhaps it kills you?

Shaken, she has buried her face in her hands. She must now try to tame her panting breath.

She quits the clinic, stares into the grayish metro crowd. The bowed silhouettes.

She sees nothing.

K.O.'d by delirium.

II

RITARDANDO A PACIERE

I am Erato, one of the muses. Perhaps the worst.

Death is not for me.

Only eternity, dismal eternity.

And only this single diversion: to obsess a human being unto death.

And then to subjugate another.

I avoid poets: they die too soon, or sink into madness.

I ruin the life of those I possess.

My prey has returned to the waiting room. I must be

silent. Or make a pretense of silence. Accord her the respite to feel once again mistress of herself. I've spoiled her life. I continue to spoil it. She can never manage to love, because no one understands the magnitude of what drives her. Poor fool, with such a naïve and fragile heart.

And her turmoil is so lamentable. Look: last spring, thanks to a newspaper contest, she won an invitation to the premiere of a play in a large hangar near the port. Six stages decorated in garish colours were surrounded by ugly wooden stands for the spectators. Accompanied by blaring music and a mix of smoke and artificial rain effects, a band of miserable actors did their best with a hermetic and pretentious script. From nearby came the river's oily, putrid breath. As she studied the sullen faces of the audience, my poor bored darling yawned, shivered, blew on her fingers, twisted a strand of her hair, crossed and uncrossed her legs. She yearned only for the end of the performance, when she could get away and relieve an imperious need to urinate. Yet, I was not obliged to manifest myself that night. A spectator behind her slipped the tip of his foot between her buttocks.

At first, she thought it was merely carelessness. She dared not budge. Minutes passed. Surely he would realize his mistake and remove his foot. He did not remove his foot. Premeditation became undeniable.

She considered various solutions. Stand up, confront this person, offer him a slap across the face and a piece of her mind, and make a dignified escape from the theatre. Except that it occurred to her that, grateful to be thus shaken from its torpor, the audience might applaud. Too embarrassing: already, in the dusty bookstore where she works part-time, the appearance of a new customer reduces her to stuttering. She could have simply pushed her neighbours over and moved. But, to her right two lovebirds entwined in embrace were indifferent to their surroundings, and to her left, an obese woman had spread herself out contentedly. Over her shoulder, she glimpsed the troublesome man's trousers. They were badly tailored in a goose-shit–coloured polyester and bagging at the knees. She could imagine the rest: a beige checked jacket and an unclean shirt the colour of wine dregs, open at the neck to reveal a fake gold medallion. The nuisance reeked of cheap cologne. Even the pointed shoe must be worn down at the heel. She lowered her eyelids. She decided that, under no circumstances would she ever want to see the boor's face. The play continued; no intermission was planned; the denouement was still a distant promise. Why had this lout selected her? Had he sensed her extreme shyness? Was it chance, or had he been eyeing her from the moment they'd entered the hangar? She despised her cowardice. Her education bogged down in the rules of decorum. The fact, finally, of being born a woman, and thus compelled to endure the insults of every Tom, Dick and Harry.

But shouldn't she get some pleasure out of the situation instead? She smiled at the thought. The melodrama was dragging on before an increasingly hostile public. Why not transform her suffering into self-satis-faction? She edged back on her seat imperceptibly. Millimetre by millimetre. Until the small of her back was pressing against the oaf's tibia. The shoe had disappeared beneath her. Beneath the thin cloth of her skirt, she felt the idiot's clodhopper, the double lacing, the hump of the toes. By turning her knees and thighs inward, she was able to unfold the leaves of her pudenda and bring her clitoris up against the curve of the gunboat. She thrust her hand under her loose sweater to finger an areola, she rolled the quickly hardening nipple between thumb and index finger. Her lips parted slightly to receive an invisible kiss. With only the slightest effort, she obtained more pleasure than anyone else in the hangar that night, pleasure enhanced by its being secret. She fled during the final bows. And has never returned to the theatre since, for fear of meeting the creep. Too bad for her.

Nevertheless, in the following weeks, rage thundered within her, rage at having been passive, rage against her own inability to protest, to defend herself. This feeling was amplified by a racket of disastrous memories, aggressions in the night, odious harassment, more or less severe abuse. To calm her, I suggested blood-soaked and implacable fantasies. She plunged into them shamelessly. Visions of naked men stretched in chains, their ankles crushed in Spanish gaiters, their wrists locked alongside their necks in violin-shaped pillories strung with bells; with the glacial determination of vengeance, she took hold of the flesh-ripping iron spider from the glowing brands of a brazier, glorified in the horrible screams, delighted in the sickening spluttering of grilled wounds. She tortured slowly. After several weeks of these consensual nightmares, she was overcome by nausea. Then peace. I had to resort to some new tactic.

Here she is, in the waiting room, blowing her nose.

Her breathing is still difficult. She rummages in her outmoded handbag for her anti-asthma inhaler. She fires two shots into her throat and reflects how often, after making love, she had to use this damned pump to relieve her suffocation. Love. Once. Long ago.

She stares at the dozing alkie, a droplet of snot dangling from his nose. She starts. Can this be him, the filmmaker who disappeared a dozen years ago; everyone thought he'd gone into exile, been interned, committed suicide? How she loved his films, their violent poetry…. She studies the bum more closely, thinks she recognizes the curve of the bushy eyebrows. Here's a fine hook to dig into your lip, my spiny stickleback.

You were in your early twenties. Hypnotized by this particular director's productions; you'd sit for days on end in the first row of the theatre, reduced to a gaze submerged in the screen. The first viewing left you shaken, the tenth exalted, the fortieth — you never went back to see a film more than fifty times —

transported you into painful ecstasy. O, pitiful excess of timorous youth... Everywhere on this earth, war was rampant, atrocities were committed under protection of the law, entire peoples suffered from tyranny, but you, wrapped in your personal obsessions, paid no mind. Didn't you even write the director a wild, desperate letter, to which you attached a photograph of yourself, not even a complete picture— you were convinced you were too ugly— just the eyes? He couldn't reply, since you hadn't included your address. Thus, you awaited each new film release with all the dismay of unrequited love, sitting through your fifty viewings like a doomed passion. This was for me a period of idleness: I had little to do to transport you outside reality.

And so it was, that winter ten years ago, that you resolved suddenly, in spite of your asthma and allergies, to buy a cat to cheat your solitude. It was a blizzarding Monday: the city had gone to ground under the assaults of the cold, schools and businesses had almost all abdicated, while downtown only a few oblique silhouettes leaned into the bombardment of gravel-like snow. Muffled up to your neck, you took the precaution of covering your nose and mouth in a woolen scarf matching your hat, so as not to suffocate in the frozen north wind. The winter storm powdered your lashes and drew tears from your eyes. You were painfully struggling towards home holding the kitten in one hand under the collar of your fur coat, when you remembered you'd run out of cigarettes. You rushed into the first establishment that was still open, an elegant restaurant from which, in less drastic weather, your timidity would have barred you. The heat inside, like a swig of whisky, set your head spinning. They must have been short of staff: some tables had not been cleaned. The scent of food cooked in wine hovered languidly. You had already paid the harried waiter for your cigarettes when a man slumped at the bar called your name. Dumbfounded, you recognized your adored filmmaker! And hope erupted within you, the hope that your dull life might swing, had swung — hope has always been among my greatest allies — you were submerged in shining images of balls and ovations! travel and triumph! whirlpools of pleasure and luxury! You had to fight not to faint.

But you had to act fast. Catch your luck in flight. Was it really you, or rather me, who spoke in a hoarse voice, a voice that came from the belly: "Follow me"? You began to move immediately toward the street. Your heart was an eagle trapped in a net. On your way, you filched a serrated knife from a plate on which had gelled a pinkish sauce. Outside, winter roared, unrelenting, pitiless. You ventured into the nearest alley. Against your throat, the raging animal mewed. You checked behind to see if the director had obeyed your command. Yes, he was hard on your heels, hurriedly buttoning his coat. You took refuge next to a garbage container stinking of rust and moldy food. The raptor between your ribs struggled like one possessed. Frantic and

breathless, the man finally caught up. You showed him
the knife. He paled: did he suspect a trap? The revenge
of a crazed fan? Behind your scarf you smiled: puny you,
a threat!... You ordered him to take the knife. Discon-
certed, almost dazed, he took it: what did you want him
to do? Stab you? Slit the cat's throat? Solemnly, like a
priestess conducting a ritual, with one hand you unfas-
tened your coat and raised your long plaid skirt. You
told him to cut your wool tights. As the elastic at the
waist was tough and the mesh tightly knit, the filmmaker
had to work hard, and his fingers soon stiffened round
the handle. The snow whipped you both relentlessly.
In a neighbouring street, an ambulance siren modulated
its funereal song. What tragedy would soon be unveiled:
heart attack, accident, fire? Your panties yielded more
easily. The cold rushed between your legs. The director
dropped the knife at your feet and quickly unzipped his
fly. His penis, a brilliant scarlet, seemed to brave the
blizzard's ferocity.

The man raised one of your thighs and, in one fell swoop, entered you. You were only partially surprised by your dampness, you felt a bird take flight between your breasts, could it be that one only had to express one's desire for it to be consummated? The director, bracing his hands against the leprous wall behind you, had begun to pound you, to roughly excavate you, when the cat managed to free itself and leapt at his face. You tried to grab the creature, but the filmmaker was quicker, seizing it and flinging it to the ground so brutally that it was almost knocked unconscious. Your concupiscence was extinguished. What rotten adventure had you gotten yourself into? To what were you surrendering yourself? To whom? With a force that surprised even you you freed yourself, picked up the knife, and fled without thinking about the man who had fallen in a thud against the container. The cat had scooted into the squall. You did not go far, taking refuge in the restaurant. Why did you have a strange feeling that you had never been here before? The place was empty. The tables were clean and lustrous. How could you not have noticed all these gigantic silver-veined mirrors in which emptiness echoed? Without removing your damp fur, you slid into a booth; the leatherette covered bench exhaled, fatigued. You pulled down your scarf and removed your gloves and hat. You placed the knife in front of you, and the waiter — a different waiter, much older than the other — appeared soundlessly to whisk it away with a sleight of hand. He returned with a cassis-flavoured tea, though you'd not said a word. Did you hear the moving strains of the "Lacrimosa" from Mozart's *Requiem*, or was it the mere memory of it that moved you to tears? Did you toss your panties and wool tights in the garbage of the washroom? Did you smoke every last one of your cigarettes? And later, once the blizzard had finally died down, in the creamy silence of the city decked out in its best Sunday whites, wasn't every trace of your and his footsteps erased? I was beginning to enjoy myself! The following week, a nasty fever kept you in bed and, in your ravings, you struggled to remember every detail: the feline's Spanish coat, the man's bushy eyebrows, the shape of his effulgent cock, all with less and less certainty, so that, after all, hadn't you invented the entire incident? Or rather, had you whispered it to yourself with such determination that it became a part of your past?

Nothing, absolutely nothing pleases me more than when you lose your footing in your memory!

But are you suddenly thinking? The subway is grumbling three feet away. You want to throw yourself under its wheels!

You want to die!

Excuse me!

I'll shut up!

Don't move.

Wait. It's all true! Wait...

III

MORENDO

The taste of pig-iron in her teeth. Outside the clinic, she leans over a well encircled by a fibro-cement guard rail. Five metres below, the subway rails run between platforms. Not high enough. She runs a little further, to another well above the second subway line. Here, the fall would be at least twelve metres. A train pulls out of the station. She calculates the time between trains: by her watch, seven minutes, forty-one seconds. Her determination is steadfast. What is she giving up that is so wonderful? A glum childhood under an authoritarian mother's heel... an unsatisfying job... six minutes. One day, during her schoolgirl years, she wet her panties in a fit of giggles; the sister rinsed them in the hallway drinking fountain, and hung them above the green blackboard; the "long-sleeved" underpants — sewn by her widowed mother out of the chestnut brown wool of a threadbare garment — had provided amusement to her young schoolmates for weeks. Why does this memory suddenly rear up now, if not to underscore the complete failure of such an anodyne life, her life... Two minutes. No one will miss her. She has no one to miss. At most, she feels an imperceptibly faint regret for those who will presently witness her annihilation. In the middle of the afternoon, the herd is thin and slow. A dozen shrivelled old men, a scattering of idle schoolboys, a few immigrants, cold and exhausted. There's even a small beige puppy, imperturbable, in the bag of a woman standing and reading at the edge of the platform. Does she sense she's being watched? She closes her book, puts it away under her dog, considers, to her left a starchy middle-aged woman steeped in her troubles, then to her right an indigo-crested ephebe contemplating his calcium-stained cowboy boots. At last she lifts her gaze. Has she recognized, or does she identify with, the woman above, gripping the steel railing with both hands? Sixty terrible seconds pass. The woman with the dog waves to her, her fingers spread, the hint of a smile. A simple mark of sympathy, erased by the subway's arrival.

Patience now once again, seven minutes and forty-one seconds. There's nothing left to meditate. Nor kindness to remember. Nor disappointments to drink down to the dregs. Nothing. Horizon zero.

She tenses, for it's always in moments like these that the Voice torments her. But...! No humming Voice! Not a chirp! Not a warble! This silence... is it possible... yes! This quiet... like a seabed far from the world!

Ah! She can breathe more freely. From one of the

halls she can hear an accordion playing. Such a happy tune. This peace... Why seek death, now that I...?

I? For the first time, I... Since the Voice is silent!... I enter the clinic. Waiting will be tougher now... The woman behind the counter smiles at me. Nicely... She asks how I am. Yes. Very well. Thank you... I won't tell her that I've never felt better in twenty years... I have been delivered! The Voice... Don't think of that. I'm at peace, now... I'm normal, now... Mustn't forget to pick up milk at the store... I like having such ordinary stuff to think about... Being bored... Hey! To celebrate, later I'll buy myself that ivory blouse... If I'm not too late... Pretty, the grey on these walls... Easy on the eyes... That boy sitting in front, so nervous, he must be seventeen, eighteen years old... A foreigner, Chilean, or Brazilian... Not bad looking, really... A man's hands, the way I like them, square... Those hands, around my waist, or on my breasts... And that hair, so thick, it would tickle my thighs... Not difficult at all, daydream-

ing on my own... No wild ravings... What a relief...
Without batting an eyelash, the receptionist hands his
file back to the South American, saying: "Ginette
Ladouceur, you're next." A woman's name?! But
how...? Oh, I get it: that's why his medical insurance
card is so badly battered; because so many people use
it... He must be an illegal immigrant. The clinic treats
them anyway; not all doctors are swine... He's walking
past me, the bulge of his rod just by my face... I
wouldn't mind getting to know that boy... Impossible.
I wouldn't dare... And, his poverty... He must live with
his parents, twelve people in a three-and-a-half room
apartment... It would be too complicated... Not the
place... Nor the right era, for that matter... Once upon
a time...

A few centuries ago, maybe... Yes, yes, that's it...
In the jungle... In South America... Before the dicta-
tors... Before Columbus... I... I was born an albino,
ashen-skinned: *Pire krembu*... My own mother would

have cast me out in disgust... According to tradition, they should have broken open my skull, boiled and eaten me... Instead, they left me on the ground... To escape the evil eye, the camp left immediately to settle elsewhere... A one-eyed, practically bald sorceress took me in... She had no heir... Or she took pity on me... She taught me the mysteries of mushrooms, roots, herbs and tree saps... Potions, poisons and perfumes... Among other things, the recipe for a dye of limes and mashed cochineal to protect me from the sun, a carmine paste I spread over my body... But my protector also taught me the art of making arrows, and fire... O double sacrilege... She drowned a dozen moons after my first menstruation... I was old enough to take care of myself... Solitude among the sweltering teaks and mangroves... the delights of *feijoa* and sugar cane... raptures of the tanager and umbrella cockatoo's song... Four jaguars accompanied me everywhere... One night, under cover of darkness, they surrounded me... Have been with me ever since... I don't know why... The absence of odour, maybe... I have no odour... Never have had... No smell... By the huts, in the fire's glow, terrifying tales are told... About me and my four wild cats!...

I am feared... No one will bother me again...

I like to spy on the males of the tribe... Trail them through the *igapos* and swamps... Once, in the lianas of a *pindo*, I discovered a hunter masturbating... Nearby, a band of screaming monkeys were howling...

The sun was at its deadly zenith. Clouds of mist undulated across the ground like *laos*... The chirring of the insects alone was deafening... The jaguars and I had torn up a *sapajou* to snack on... I got the still warm and palpitating liver, and, with the taste still on our lips, we were lounging in some fallen underbrush... One of the big cats noticed a gentle oscillation among the creepers... I stopped him with a hand sign. Noiselessly, I made my way up to a perch just above the man... The triangular scarifications on his cheeks meant he'd already killed... Better to remain undiscovered... But, eyes almost shut, he was completely engrossed. In his masturbation. I was fascinated by the length, the breadth of his *embo*. By the relentless hand rhythm. By the gland, pointing, impatient. My blood pounded in my ears... Drowning out all the crackling, the yelping, the sighing of the jungle... By my head, a lizard, scarlet anole, snapped up a praying mantis occupied in the performance of her devotions... The hand was going wild. The gland turned violet. Finally the man reared up. Sprayed. Streams of honey. The acrid scent. So mysterious. I had to taste it. With all my might. This liquid between my legs. This blaze between my thighs.

At the new moon, luck smiled down on me. A mother was giving birth; from the beginning of time, the men were forbidden to witness a birthing; my hunter, returning from an expedition and shouldering a large peccary, stepped right into the midst of the gathering of silent women; crying out in terror, they threw up their arms to cover their faces, while he, appalled, dropped his catch and vanished back into the forest. He was now under the curse of *pane* — bad luck in hunting. He must, to be released, kill an animal before the next dawn. The jaguars and I slipped away, all danger and desire...

I had concocted a hillside trap, a cave whose entrance I'd camouflaged. Taking turns whimpering as though they were wounded, my cats drew the warrior, caught up in the phantom chase, toward the trap... With one well-aimed arrow, I nailed his quiver to the trunk of a twisted fig tree... He tripped and fell into my trap! He was mine!!

The most powerful of the jaguars stood guard. All that remained was for my captive, ravaged by hunger, to swallow what I had prepared for him: a succulent guava, or one of the squirming and sweetened *mynda* larvae, all poisoned by me: he would then fall into a trance resembling death...

The shroud of night descended. My throat dry, I entered the grotto, and thrust my torch in the sand. A swarm of screeching bats scattered. My dangerous sweets were all gone. Was my prisoner dead?

He seemed to be sleeping, huddled under his blanket of sisal. With great care, I uncovered him. He was still breathing. I was struck once more by the coarse beauty of his able hunter's body, the roundness of his rump, the sturdiness of his neck... Between his thighs two plump testicles nested. I scratched gently between his scapulae, then tickled his ribs, and even plunged a finger between his teeth. His palate, the pointed canines, the mucous membranes in his cheeks, nothing escaped my attention. My sleeper did not react, except for a soft sucking of his lips when my index pulled out of his mouth. A swamp welled up in me.

I turned my warrior on his back. Knelt down. I

fought so hard to restrain my craving that I drew blood from my lip. His sex, its fruits swelling so close to my face: this enigma demanded my caress. A single breath and it unfurled, a flick of my tongue and it awakened, dilated. I swallowed him all at once, accentuating the transformation, the miracle. A quick, too quick pump, and that mouthful, already, with its brackish, savage flavour, which did not quench my curiosity…

Seven times that night I tired myself out ravaging my warrior's barbarous honey. My palms, my breasts, my hair, the entire cave, the jungle herself were drenched in it. At dawn, I emerged, panting and marked by the man's odour. The four jaguars growled their disapproval, to death…

— *Open your eyes, my little worm. Welcome to the waiting room.*

Oh! How divinely you amuse me! Did you think you'd eliminated me with your pathetic suicide threat?

I am a virus in your blood, your brain, undetectable venom in your soul, infecting every fibre of your being, and no drug, not even electroshock, could rid you of me! You're not even clever enough to decipher my simplest stratagem... For you, I will have as many voices as there are drops of water in all the seas, and more tales than humanity has ever told. A measly imagination, a stunted logic, pathetic emotions, the mediocrity of a flightless destiny — such is your lot without me. Why this stubborn determination to refuse me?

Wipe your tears, blow your nose, at last the doctor will see you now, go....

IV

LEGATO CON CRESCENDO

At last, you are called, by a masculine voice, a bass, and a whitecap swells up inside you, you push the consulting room door, the doctor is there, standing by his desk, Mozart playing in the background, the windowless walls papered from ceiling to floor in a photograph of a forest of sequoias, jades, golds and bronzes, the man neither speaks nor bats an eyelash, and your gaze in his, a gaze shaded by blond eyelashes, very straight, very long, a child's lashes, a gaze of blue-green irises, washed out, softened by too many tears, tears in vain, tears shed over all the destitution, all the distress, you have this intuition, this man has loved more than been loved, the moment's immobility, the bolt of desire, that impulse within you, wanting to touch the bare chest of this man, that impulse, that source slicing through rock, and almost in spite of yourself, your right hand slowly abandons your left hand, unfolds carefully, as though it were afraid of frightening a sparrow, but without trembling, your fingers already in the fold of his smock, harsh cloth, while attentive, not in the least annoyed, the doctor, who has followed your right hand's movement toward his belt without the slightest smile, once more rivets his gaze to yours (at the very instant that, outside the clinic, by the subway booth, a red-headed student smooches with his girlfriend), and you sense that, perhaps, your boldness will be permitted, your every move encouraged, now here's your left hand near his hand, which does not shy away, which even offers the warmth of its palm, your fingers enlace, by a delicate twist of the wrist he pulls you toward him, now you're only centimetres apart, subtle exhalation of vetiver, and thyme, and your heart reels a little further (on one of the subway platforms, beneath the clinic, a grandmother pecks her granddaughter), your right hand has moved up to the collar of his shirt, undoing the top button, your index finger glances over the slight hollow at the base of his neck, a few scatterbrained hairs bristle, the skin pinks (outside, seven streets down from here, in a dive renting by the hour, on boulevard Saint-Laurent, some good-for-nothing is banging his favourite, a whore as biting as January), the second button is out of its buttonhole, and suddenly a troubling memory, very private, inadmissible, the summer of your seventh year, your mitt lodged in your mother's fleshless paw, noon in the dust of a camping site along the highway, one hundred miserable families congregating around a waterhole, since ten o'clock a carousel of battered little cars has been rumbling above the bawling din of brats and the sea roar of road traffic, a merry-go-round run by a fairground couple, both chubby, he in moustache and worn-out tails, she in a sateen bra and shopsoiled striped pantaloons, and their toothless half-blind bear, the showman picks a tune on his banjo, while his highwire lady waltzes with the plantigrade beast, grotesquely waddling, the sweat drawing pools on her grimy back, the mustachioed boss winks tenderly at his corpulent companion and, below the musician's belly, just level with your nose, this swelling of which you are the incredulous witness, no one around you, not even your mother, seeming or wanting to see the worrying bump, is it a disease, no, for clearly the individual concerned is quite happy with it, and in you this inexplicable emotion, which you've recalled over the years, but not without confusion, as you do now face to face with this doctor, you attack the third button of his shirt, your hand suddenly swift, spidering over his torso (in a low-rent housing unit in the neighbourhood,

while her baby sleeps, a single mother welcomes her
lover the mailman, still in uniform, while she, nude but
for a pair of turquoise gloves running up to her armpits,
and he laughing, still in uniform as he's being jacked),
the rumble of a rising torrent in the man, your right
hand abducted by his left, up to his lips, a dampness
flowering between your life-line and your love-line,
just like the dampness beading between your thighs (a
kilometre away, in the back room of his convenience
store, Miserere Paradis, so named more than fifty years
ago by the sisters of the orphanage, nibbles the bitter
fleece of Adelina Beauregard, a defrocked nun ten years
his senior, his squeeze, his lady love, his very own
custodial), the doctor in front of you has lowered his
gaze, smiling, blushing, the mug of a kid cooking up
some practical joke, a diabolic scheme, oh how you
loved that look, how you loved him when he broke
away from you, by intercom told his receptionist she
could go, he'd lock up, his bass voice completely

normal, not a quiver, not an inflection to betray his intentions, a man used to concealing, a man of secrets, and now, has the magic between you been blown to bits, and has the atmosphere, moments ago crackling with electricity, solidified, as face to face now you've both come up against taboo, silly, maybe even cowardly, but within you that strange wave is reborn, and that craving thirst in your mouth, once more you press up against him, your fingers clutching at his sparkling hair, pulling his face toward yours, that kiss, pianissimo, gently gently your lips, a sfumato kiss, and yet such sparks (between the river and the Jacques-Cartier Bridge, in the entranceway of a bankrupt store, a reedy fellow is stretching the brackmard of a Black man whose name he doesn't know, and for several fragrant hours he will keep its quasi-phosphorescent soft roe in the hollow of his fist), your arms around him, his arms around you, the glacial feeling dissolves, vaporizes to the deep south, you might faint (racing toward the basement of her lover's parents' in Chibougamou, in minus sixty degrees Celsius, an adolescent straddles her father's snow-ski, she's well protected by three pairs of socks, thigh-high boots, four sweaters, lined thigh boots and gloves, a woolen beret and scarf, a three-quarters felt-lined coat — her Sunday coat — but without panties beneath her mini-skirt, her bare breech, the intense cold like a flame between her thighs), his dizzying breath, and his tongue between your teeth, you yield willingly, bumping and brushing at each other until, closing in, you bite the flesh of his mouth, sending a shudder through him (on vacation in Matamoros, by the Rio Grande del Norte, on sheets of painfully brilliant white, an American student rams a Mexican she-devil to the hilt, sucking greedily on his chum, while the latter squats on the pretty grimacing face of the *bruja*, who has clearly bewitched this pair of virgins, unless they simply im-bibed too much mescal and marijuana and fell into delinquency, in any case, that's how, later, they'll half-jokingly explain the incident to themselves), but more than the vetiver and thyme, it's his skin you want to inhale, his perspiration, you massage your cheek against his chest, slide up under his arm, chewing on it with a kind of intoxication or devotion, under the spell of nutmeg and mead (to impress his brothers, as drunk as he is, a Fumante Island shepherd sodomizes one of their herd), but, what's wrong, you're crumbling, shrivelling, you break into tears at his feet, for once, you could, without a hitch, without complication, fuck someone desire has chosen for you, you're floored by an atavistic fear, a childish panic, ridiculous, a middle-aged virgin's prudishness, foolish, foolish shame, now the man kneels beside you, consoles you, rocking you back and forth, talking of tomorrow, of there being nothing to fear from tomorrow, and of hearts slowing, he whispers to you about how some of his patients resist death, now you're almost comforted, but the yearning rises up again within you, this yearning and its undercurrents, for a moment you could believe you were invincible, invulnerable, you must lay your entire body over his, you must, you snuggle a little longer in his arms, with a push of your shoulder you destabilize him, you slump together onto the rough carpet, you sprawl in a jungle of kisses, a brush-fire of laughter in your throats, irrepressible (crammed into a locker in Tokyo's red-light district, an employee manipulates to her right and left the penises that clients have introduced into the openings of the compartment, approximately a hundred hand-jobs daily), magically, it seems, the first of your sweaters and the doctor's smock have landed near the photograph of sequoias, your body moulding his, belly against belly, and against your groin, through your clothing, that delightful tumescence, the erect harquebusier, sentinel of dreams, sacrament of boudoirs, totem of a dark and deaf deity (in Bangkok, in a cubbyhole enclosed by faded draperies, some Texan or German swine deflowers his daily acquisition, a ten-year-old girl), with your

nails you scratch out obscenities on his torso, you
enflame him further, you attack his nipples, and he,
moaning with pleasure (in a car parked on the outskirts
of Novorossisk, a fiancé, Ilya, serenades Varvara, his
bride-to-be, far from the indiscretions of their families),
time stretches on the continent of desire, each minute
a lozenge of eternity in your mouth, how did you
manage to abstain so long from fornication, doesn't this
effervescence of the blood make life worth living, your
youth is already withering away, your breasts flattening,
and yet his hands rummage under your sweaters, lifting
them up, and yet he nibbles you, fingers you (somewhere near the Aral Sea, out of sight of the adults, kids
are playing at a game of touch-your-pipi-you're-dead),
the doctor is sucking on your ear lobe, you squeeze one
of his thighs between yours, press your Venus' mount
against it (in her shower, a Madagascar housewife rubs
herself to orgasm), now he stands, carries you to the
examining table, presses you against the wall, arched

against him, kisses you wildly (in Djibouti, with his pen knife, a groom slices off the infibulation of his new wife), his fingers making their way through the folds of your round skirt, into your acrylic tights, under the elastic of your panties, to the crotch (somewhere in a casbah, three young Arabs are getting all dolled up), you seem to be swept up in the waves of your pulsing pleasure palace, groundswell, imperative, burning (in the shadows of a Calabrasion room, a young suitor feasts on the *frùtto di gioia* of his beloved), with a blustering kick, you rid yourself of your boots, but the man's fingers harden on your kernel of fruit (in Bochum, in Cluj, in Zoug, in Bodø, in Drama, in a thousand-and-one other private hells, a father is raping his daughter, or son), the buckle of his belt snaps in your hands, his fly whistles (a little too loudly, a dozen homosexuals entwined octopus-like are swaying in the back room of the Mimi-poivré, a very Parisian bar), under your long nails at last, his ballocks (the captain of the three-master moored in

Ipswich and his Montreal girlfriend drift, completely nude, toward an apotheosis), you've both dropped all your clothes, layers of your too-pale flesh, at last he enters you, at last he is delving in your garden, strangely quiet, whereas your blood is boiling, into your maelstrom, your notch, why does he have this dreamy look, why this distracted look in his eyes, what is this anger, no, this exasperation, that embraces you, roughly, with your right arm and both legs, you immobilize the doctor against you, paralyze him inside you, and he smiles without knowing what you are about to do, nor do I know what you are about to do, you chew the nail of your left auricle, you shear it down to the skin, then do the same with the nail of your ring finger, mercilessly, the index finger sacrificed in turn, then you soak each finger generously in your saliva, and suddenly you feel weak, you're faint, your neck bends backwards, wilting water lily, you beg for a kiss, which he grants you, raising himself up on his toes, your left hand now slides, slips behind his cullions, your forefinger forcing the anus, which relaxes easily, then the black gate tightens around your finger, which plunges further, electrifying, boosting the man, he arches, skewers you, rides you, and you, you...

In the far reaches of the universe, two comets come together.

Between the continents, oceanic plates grind against each other to infinity.

Drained of all his suffering, an AIDS victim expires in the arms of his lover.

Two hydrogen atoms combine with an atom of oxygen.

Immortality in our veins, fleeting light.

CODA

And if you loved him. And he you. The old story... A hundred-and-one couplings later, on a sap-laden night, you'll confide in him, admit in a whisper the terrible torture to which I have subjected you for so long, these obsessions, this incessant counterpoint to your thoughts, this river of couplings, debaucheries, orgies that I pour into your mind. The one you love will listen in silence. Then, almost apologizing for stating the obvious, he'll whisper: "Why don't you write it down?"

And so, with your pen of violet ink, you'll enslave me.

To all your desires, O, my beloved.

Montréal
January 4, 1989 — June 16, 1993